filthy RICH

NOVA MONROE

SYNOPSIS

After spending summer alone in our family vacation home in Florida, it was time to face reality. My mother had run off and married another rich jerk two months ago, and they have been celebrating their honeymoon in the south of France. I'd avoided going back to Connecticut because our home would soon be taken over by the dreaded step-siblings. I had no intention of getting to know my new family. This was my mother's fourth marriage, and I wasn't going to waste another moment getting close to someone who wouldn't be around in a few years anyway. But after I found my boyfriend Chase in bed with another woman, I needed to get out of this place. So I booked a first-class ticket back to Hell and would be home before the sun sets tomorrow.

CONTAINS: STEPBROTHER ROMANCE & VIRGIN

Filthy Rich is a novella in the *Quick and Dirty Series*. If you like a short and sweet story with instalove and a happily ever after, this book is for you. Every book in the series is completely standalone. Be warned – the sex in this is raw and taboo. It is not for the faint of heart. Now dive in, you dirty little kitten.

CONTENTS

SYNOPSIS — 5

CONTENTS — 7

ONE — 9

TWO — 13

THREE — 15

FOUR — 25

FIVE — 27

SIX — 35

SEVEN — 39

EIGHT — 43

NINE — 47

TEN — 51

ELEVEN — 57

TWELVE — 61

THIRTEEN — 67

FOURTEEN — 71

FIFTEEN — 75

SIXTEEN — 81

SEVENTEEN 87

EIGHTEEN 93

NINETEEN 97

TWENTY 105

TWENTY-ONE 111

TWENTY-TWO 117

TWENTY-THREE 123

TWENTY-FOUR 127

EPILOGUE 133

ABOUT THE AUTHOR 137

WHAT TO READ NEXT 139

<u>ONE</u>

VALERIE

I stepped off the plane just before noon. The weather was significantly colder than it had been in Florida, and I felt underdressed in my cut-off jean shorts and tank top. But at least I had a kick-ass tan to show for my vacation if nothing else.

I stepped out of the airport and flagged down a cab, desperate to get out of this overcrowded disease fest and into my oversized garden tub. At least my mother and her new husband weren't due back from their trip for another week. I had some time to settle back in and enjoy some peace and quiet before the new step-monsters began to torment me. I was miserable after leaving Chase, and all I wanted was some time to heal, and if I was lucky, maybe get laid.

The trip back to the house only took about twenty minutes, but I was exhausted. I didn't sleep at all last night; instead, I'd stayed up late to pack all of my things and cry over that cheating loser. I'd devoted two years of my life to that jerk.

I lugged my heavy bags to the front door and dropped them off just inside the entryway. I would figure out how to get them up the stairs later. Now, all I wanted was a long soak in the bathtub.

The house was quiet... too quiet. I cranked up the radio in the kitchen full blast, turning on the speakers embedded in all the rooms of the house. After kicking off my shoes, I decided to rummage through my mom's liquor cabinet. I poured a heavy dose of whiskey into a large glass and filled the rest of the cup with soda. If I was going to relax, I was going to do it right.

I took a big gulp of the harsh concoction, wincing as it burned its way down my throat. I took another long drink, finishing it off before sitting the glass on the counter and pulling my tank over my head, letting it fall to the floor.

I poured another glass and shimmied out of my shorts, leaving on my white cotton panties. I loved being home alone. But, I would need to get my own place soon. Chase and I planned on buying a home after we got married. Should have known that wasn't going to happen. I took a long drink from my glass and sat it back on the counter, singing loudly to the pop song the flowed through the speakers in each room.

I decided now was the time for my soak, and I headed upstairs, desperate to scrub off any scent of Chase. I padded into my bedroom and made my way into my bathroom suite. Turning on the tub and set it to just the right temperature. I danced and sang at the top of my lungs as I slid my panties over my hips and stepped out of them. I grabbed my ponytail holder and pulled it free from my long dark hair, running my fingers through it until it laid smooth down my chest.

Turning off the tub's faucet, I slowly stepped inside, lowering myself deep into the warm water. I let my eyes fall closed as I laid back against the hard porcelain of the tub.

TWO

DAMIEN

The moment I stepped inside the sprawling mansion, I knew something was wrong. There were shoes on the floor, sexy little kitten heels, and a bottle of whiskey on the counter. Music was blaring, and even though I called out to ask if someone was here, no one responded over the song that pumped throughout the house. I thought about grabbing a weapon, but I wouldn't need one to defend myself. I'd been in the military for years and had just returned from a deployment. I was the weapon.

But there was no way this was a robbery. Either Mrs. Watson came home early from vacation, or this was someone familiar with the family.

I trudged up the sprawling staircase, listening as the sound of a young female sang along with the shitty song that was threatening to make me go deaf.

I made my way down the long hallway, stopping at the door of a room I hadn't explored. It was wide open, and a faint light was glowing from further inside, perhaps from the bathroom.

I pushed the door open wider, crossing one foot over the other like I'd learned from having to explore buildings that may house enemy combatants. But there was no one on the sprawling four-post bed.

I made my way in a little further, nearly tripping over my own feet, when I saw a sunkissed brunette in the oversized tub, her perky tits bobbing above the bubbles. My cock instantly went hard as I stopped to watch her momentarily, stunned by how absolutely gorgeous she was.

I walked closer as her legs came into view, knees bent, and she was rubbing them together like she wanted to get off. I ran my tongue over my lips, my mouth suddenly dry.

THREE

VALERIE

I grabbed my bath scrunchie and poured a healthy dose of vanilla bath scrub onto it, and began to slowly rub it over myself. I massaged the silky liquid over my breasts, the rough netted material scratching lightly over my pink nipples, causing them to harden. I ran the rough material down my stomach, aching for a release that I had gone too long without.

My hand slipped lower over my bare mound, dipping between my legs as I pushed it against my folds. I sucked my lower lip between my teeth as I rotated my hips against my hand, loving the rough pressure. With my eyes closed, I could almost imagine it was the prickly stubble of a beard.

"I could help you with that," A deep voice called out over the music, and my eyes flew open as I tried to cover myself and search for something I could use as a weapon against an intruder.

"Get out of my house now before I call the police," I screeched as I sat up, sloshing water over the side of the tub. My eyes fell on the guy who was probably a few years older than me, mid-twenties, with dark, messy hair that looked like he'd just ran his fingers through it and a five o'clock shadow with a devilish grin. I felt the blush creep over my entire body, and the glint in his eyes let me know he saw every single inch.

"I should say the same to you. I live here. You're lucky I don't call the police or...." His head cocked to the side as his gaze drifted lower, "I could lend you a hand." He winked.

"You don't live here, you nutcase. This is my home."

He shook his head as he took a few steps closer and sank down to his knees next to me. I could smell his cologne, a mixture of cigarettes and musk. It was so incredibly male.

"I live here, doll. I have for a few weeks, and I have never seen you around. I'm sure I would have noticed." His eyes drifted over my body once more, and I almost came from his eye-fucking. "The owner,

Pam Watson, she personally invited me to stay here, and she had never mentioned you."

I rolled my eyes as I sat up, the cold air instantly hardening my nipples again as the water sloshed out towards his feet, but he didn't move.

"Pam is my mother. I'm Valerie." I felt like I was shrinking under his intense gaze. It wasn't odd for my mom to lend out the place when she wasn't around. She hardly stayed at this property, and it was a vacation dream spot.

"You don't mind if I call her and verify your story, do you?" His eyes narrowed, and I did the same, wanting to smack him. I didn't want my mother to know I was back home. She would know something was wrong with Chase and me. I wasn't in the mood to explain how I had let *the best thing to ever happen to me* slip through my fingers. My mother was the one that hooked us up. She wanted to make sure her daughter ended up with *one of our own kind,* as she put it, which was code for *filthy rich*. Our relationship had been doomed from the start. I never felt like I had much in common with Chase besides money.

"Don't you dare," I bit back, hoping my tone sounded threatening enough.

"Ohhh... you're hiding out."

"No." I folded my arms over my chest, knowing how ridiculous I must look sitting in front of this sexy stranger with no clothes on.

"You're secret is safe with me, princess." He winked again, and I hated the pulse of pleasure that shot down between my legs. The warmth of the liquor began to flow through me now, and there was little I cared about at the moment. The steady clenching between my legs hadn't ebbed, and I was in desperate need of release.

"I'm not a princess." I rolled my eyes and sank back down, laying back against the edge of the tub. I hated the way I was judged in this town. I wasn't like those other girls who vacationed in the Hamptons and lived for their next shopping spree.

"Whatever you say, Princess." He laughed, and my eyes shot open.

"My *name* is Valerie."

"I'm Damien," he replied with a smile, deep dimples in his cheeks. I melted like butter against the side of the tub.

"How long are you crashing here?" I asked, my teeth pressing into my lower lip.

"Not long. I'm on leave. I'll be heading back to base soon."

"Soldier boy? I never would have guessed with that haircut," I replied dryly. He laughed, but I could tell he was too preoccupied with my naked body to offer a retort.

"Damien..." His name rolled off my tongue, and I wondered what it would be like to moan it. "Do you think you could scrub my back for me?" I rolled over, bowing my back to push my ass up a little. He sucked in a ragged breath and grabbed the bath scrunchie that floated through the water.

"Who am I to turn down a beautiful lady like yourself?" He asked, his voice gruff, as he grabbed the body wash and poured it over the netted washcloth. His hand dipped into the warm water, and he began to rub small, gentle circles over my back. I let my eyes fall closed, reveling in the sensation of his touch.

"Lower," I asked bravely as the alcohol began to lessen my inhibitions. His hand dipped lower, roaming over the globes of my ass.

"Valerie," he said in a husky tone. I knew he was having reservations about what was happening, but I didn't care. All I could think about was Chase on the beach with that bimbo. I needed a release.

"Lower," I repeated. Damien slipped his hand lower the tips of his fingers, sliding free from the scrunchie and brushing against my ass cheek. Goosebumps followed in their wake.

"Valerie, I can't do this."

I raised my ass, lifting up on my knees, giving him a full view of my smooth pussy from behind. I wanted more than anything to just have fun and get fucked. *Why was he making this so difficult?*

"You have no idea what you're asking."

"I'm not that drunk." I laughed, irritated that he was telling me no. It wasn't something I was used to nor liked. "Fine." I rolled over onto my back. My hand slid down over my breast and dipped between my legs. His eyes smoldered as he watched my finger slip between my folds and stroke gentle circles over my clit. I loved the idea of being watched. It had been a fantasy of mine for years, but a woman of my upbringing never talked of such things. In fact, a woman of my upbringing never had fun at all. My sex life generally consisted of lying on the bed while Chase ate me out, and I'd have to go finger myself later to get off or him ramming his dick down my throat and cumming on my tits after three pumps. We'd never gone all the way. We were waiting until we got married. Well, *I* was waiting. He clearly was not. But just because we hadn't done the deed didn't mean I was a prude. We'd tried just about everything else together. It just clearly wasn't enough for him.

The only time I orgasmed was on my own. I was an expert at it by this point and could cum as quickly as I pleased. But today, I didn't want to get off as fast as possible. Instead, I wanted to enjoy those dark green eyes that raked over my body as I slipped a finger inside of myself and began to ride it.

Damien pulled his shirt over his head and let it fall to the floor. He was built like a rock star, with his ab muscles perfectly defined. I let my eyes drift lower and watched his hands as they fumbled with the button of his jeans. Finally, he pulled the zipper down, and his heavy cock sprang free. He was several inches bigger than Chase, the only man I had ever seen naked in real life. The size frightened and excited me. He wrapped his fingers around the base of his thick cock and slowly began stroking himself as precum leaked from the tip. I moved my finger inside of myself in time with his movements, imagining what it would be like to ride him.

My pussy clenched around my finger, wishing it was him inside of me. My back bowed, pushing my tits out of the soapy water toward him. He sunk down to his knees, continuing to grip his cock tightly in one hand as he reached out and ran the palm of his free hand over one of my breasts.

"Maybe we should wash each other," he said as his hand slid over my belly and dipped over my mound. I continued to fuck myself as his fingers slid over mine, and I nodded my head in agreement.

"Nothing wrong with that," I replied as I slipped a second finger into my tight hole.

Damien stood, shoving his jeans down to the floor and kicking them off before stepping into the warm water and lowing himself beside me. He lay on his side as his right hand began to glide over my stomach. I reached beside myself with my free hand and wrapped my fingers around the thick base of his cock. It was so smooth and hard at the same time. I slowly began to stroke him, twisting my wrist with each rise of my hand. His fingers trailed lower, finding my clit just beneath the surface of the water. He rubbed his rough fingertip against the hardened nub as he leaned over and pulled my puffy nipple into his mouth before two of his large fingers pushed inside of me roughly.

I cried out as my body stretched around him. Damien began to push deeper inside of me. "Your pussy is so tight."

"Your fingers are so big it hurts," I whimpered as I pushed my hips down on him, grinding against his palm. "You should kiss it and make it better," I whispered as I stuck my lower lip out in a mock pout. The left side of his mouth rose in a lopsided grin, and his eyes narrowed. Then, suddenly, his hand withdrew, and he leaned away from me, leaving me momentarily worried I'd offended him.

"Stand," he demanded. The water sloshed as I pushed to my shaky feet, wholly exposed to his narrowed gaze. He ran his tongue out over his lower lip, and I couldn't help but let out a heavy sigh, desperate for his mouth to be against my flesh. Finally, he sat up in front of me, inches from my mound, gazing up at me before the flat of his tongue pressed against my clit, causing my knees to buckle. He chuckled, grabbing my legs and holding them steady before his tongue was against me again, pushing hard over my clit before spreading my folds to delve deeper. "You taste like honey." His palms ran over my ass, gripping the globes and forcing me to stay pressed tightly against his mouth as he lapped at my juices.

I placed a hand on either side of his head as I began to rock my hips against his face. He moaned, and the vibration from his mouth sent me tumbling over the edge. His tongue never slowed as pulse after pulse of pleasure rippled through my body.

FOUR

DAMIEN

Fuck. I have never tasted anything as sweet as Valerie's cunt. I wanted more. I was desperate for it. I held her against my mouth, delving my tongue in and out of her, lapping up every sweet drop of cream she would give me.

I moved my mouth back to her clit, flicking my tongue against it lightly and causing her stomach muscles to clench as she started to ride my face again.

"What are you doing?" she panted.

"I'm going to make you cum again," I groaned, latching myself back onto her. Her skin was a light brown like she spent hours out laying in the sun, but the inside of her cunt was pale pink. It looked so inviting and tasted so fucking good. I didn't care who she was or why she was here.

My cock was rock hard, and begging to stretch her out and make her mine. But after I had fingered her, I knew I'd really have to work my way up to fucking her the way my body begged me to. I wasn't a gentle man. I wasn't the kind of guy who would make love to you and give you flowers. I liked to fuck, and the dirtier, the better.

Right now, having this spoiled little princess riding my face was as close to heaven as I could get without pounding my cock into her until I filled her with my cum. Her body rocked against me, and she whimpered as I held her captive, eating her like she was my last fucking meal.

Her fingernails bit into my flesh, and I knew she would leave marks, but that only made me hungrier. Her body began to shake, and I let out a growl as I lapped up her juices, delving my tongue inside of her as she rode it through another release.

FIVE

VALERIE

My mouth hung open as I panted, struggling to catch my breath as he pulled back from me, looking up as if he was still hungry. Then, rising to his feet, his cock was hard and ready between us. His fingers fisted in my hair as my hands fell to his chest. I could feel the head of his cock pressed against my overly sensitive clit. My pleasure was soon overtaken by fear. I'd never even known a man could be that large, and I didn't know if my body could handle him.

"You scared?" he asked as the side of his mouth curved up in a devious smirk.

"No," I spat back like a brat. That only caused his grin to widen, and anger bubbled inside of me. Chase was out screwing God knows who, and I was too much of a chicken to lose my V-card. And now, this totally hot guy was laughing at me. So, I did what I do best. I took a shot at him. "But I don't fuck poor people."

That wiped the smirk from his face. "Are you fucking kidding me?" he asked with his massive cock still fisted in his hand.

I shook my head as I stepped out of the tub, leaving wet footprints behind as I sauntered out of the room.

Every bone in my body felt like it had turned to jelly. I'd never had an orgasm rip through my body so fast and so fierce before. But the second his cock was ready to push inside of me, I ran away scared. I could tell by the look on his face he was absolutely livid by the way I left him, but I couldn't tell him I didn't know how to handle someone his size.

Thankfully, I had the presence of mind to grab my robe before fleeing to the kitchen to pour myself another drink. Damien wasn't far behind, his hard chest still dripping, and his jeans were slung low on his hips, revealing those delicious V muscles that lead down to his massive cock.

"What the fuck was that?" he snapped.

I rolled my eyes, finishing off my drink before setting the glass down on the counter. "What?" I asked with a shrug.

"You begged me to get you off, and you just walk away without helping me out?"

"Helping you with what?" I asked, feigning ignorance, but my eyes betrayed me as they dipped fractionally.

"Do you need me to show you again?" he asked, grabbing his crotch crudely.

"No thanks," I replied coolly as I refilled my cup.

Damien narrowed his eyes, bitting out the word, "Fine." Before disappearing through the formal dining room.

"That was easy enough," I mumbled to myself as I pulled open the fridge and rummaged around for something to snack on. I settled on a salad that had to be Damien's, but I didn't really care.

I sank down on a stool at the island, eating away at my food, singing along to the song playing over the radio. As I ate, I scrolled through my social media, stalking my ex and his new fuckbuddy, periodically stopping to drown my sorrows in liquor.

The sound of a giggle in the distance pulled me from my self-loathing, and I pushed from my chair, stumbling as I retied my robe and set out to find who had made that noise.

Damien laid on a chaise lounge next to the pool. From my view, all I could see was his muscular arms as his hands laced underneath his head. I slipped out of the open door to ask if he had guests when I was stopped from the sight of a bottled blonde bobbing her head up and down over his crotch.

"What are you doing?" I slurred, with my hands thrown in the air. I had no right to be mad at Damien. He wasn't my boyfriend who'd cheated on me. I was the one who had turned him down. But how the hell could he go from eating me out to letting some other girl suck his dick in a matter of minutes.

Damien glanced over at me, smirking. "This is my friend…" his voice trailed off. He didn't even know her name.

The girl lifted her mouth from his cock and smiled over at me. "Britney," she finished for him.

"Pleasure," I snapped.

"Pleasures all mine," Damien shot back.

I felt my cheeks heat as I bit back a curse. "Damien, can we have a word, please?"

Tucking his length back in his pants, he whispered something to Britney before pushing from his chair. I shuffled back inside of the house, with Damien following close behind me.

"What are you doing?" I asked as I spun to face him.

"Getting my dick sucked. Does that bother you, princess?"

I rolled my eyes. "Actually, it does. I don't think my mother would appreciate you bringing your whores here and corrupting her impressionable young daughter."

"Should we also tell your mommy how you rode my face?" Damien barked out a laugh. "Go ahead and call her. I'll wait."

I felt my face blister red. He knew I didn't want her to know I was back home.

"Better yet, *you* can finish me off, and we can call it even."

"As if I would touch your dick after it has been in *her* mouth."

"You had your chance, princess," he replied with a shrug before turning and heading back outside to an eager Britney. Only this time, he didn't lay down. Instead, he stood, facing the massive wall of windows I was behind, and guided her to her knees so he could stare at me as she took his length down her throat.

I propped my hands on my hips angrily, glaring at him. But he didn't look the least bit phased. In fact, he looked like he was enjoying himself... a lot. Now my cheeks were heating for a different reason.

I turned and stormed back to the kitchen island, climbing up one of the stools and sitting on top of the countertop with my legs spread toward him. I undid the tie of my robe, letting it fall down my arms as my eyes locked back onto his.

His mouth hung open in shock as I let my fingers slide down over my stomach and over my dripping wet pussy. I began to rub my clit, spreading my lips and allowing my fingers to slip lower, rubbing over my hole that was still sore from the intrusion of his fingers.

Gripping Britney's hair, he began to fuck her face harder, his eyes locked on my pussy that was dripping with need. *What was wrong with me?* I was supposed to be making him jealous, and instead, I was getting turned on. *Really* turned on.

I began to rub over my clit eagerly, desperate to chase the high I had after he had eaten me out.

SIX

DAMIEN

I was rock fucking hard and choking the shit out the poor girl with my cock shoved down her throat. Staring at Valerie up on the counter with her legs spread looked like a meal I was desperate to devour. But I'd already made her cum twice, and she'd left me high and dry. I wasn't going to let her screw me over again. So instead, I gripped onto Britney's hair, holding her still as I fucked her face. A tear streamed down her cheek, but she continued to suck me off like it was what she was born to do.

Valerie dipped a finger between her pink lips and began to fuck herself, riding her hand as her palm pressed against her clit. I rocked my hips in time with hers. She may have been trying to piss me off, but I could tell she was on the verge of cumming, and my dirty little girl liked watching me fuck some random chick's mouth, knowing I was thinking of her.

I cursed myself in my head. She wasn't *my* dirty girl. Not yet. But judging by how she kept her pussy wet around me, it was only a matter of time. I could still taste her honey on my lips, still feel the way her pussy clenched around my tongue as she came, desperate to be filled.

Slipping a second finger inside of herself, she threw her head back, lost in her own fantasy of us. I felt my balls tightened, and my cock thickened as Valerie raised her head, her eyes locking on mine with her mouth wide.

I shot my load down Britney's throat as she happily milked my heavy cock for every drop. Valerie raised her fingers and licked her own cream from them, causing more cum to leak out of me.

I quickly tucked my cock back in my pants before guiding Britney, some random chick from a hookup app, to the side gate of the yard so I could get rid of her.

I stalked back inside of the house to see Valerie flat on her back, knees still up and spread wide, relaxing after her fingerfucking session. She sighed, clearly pleased with her show.

"What's that?" I asked, going to the plastic container beside her. She glanced over before shrugging.

"Salad."

"That was my dinner."

"I thought I was your dinner," she replied with a fake pout. I was going to lose my fucking mind if this little girl didn't learn some serious fucking manners. I grabbed her thighs and yanked her toward the edge of the counter.

"What the hell are you doing?" she squealed as I positioned her pussy before me.

"You ate my salad. Now I'm going to toss yours."

"What –" she started as I bent down and ran my tongue over her milky slit. Her back bowed off the granite, and a shudder ran through her body.

"Shut the fuck up like a good girl, and I will make you cum again after I clean up the mess you made." I began to eat her like I was ravenous, and she let her legs fall to the sides, her hand threading through my hair to hold me against her. But she didn't need to worry. There was nothing that could make me stop lapping up every drop of pleasure from her little cunt.

After I'd cleaned her up and sucked on her clit just enough to make her legs quiver, I pulled away. "Flip over," I ordered.

SEVEN

VALERIE

I pushed up on my elbows to look at him, confused by his request, and apparently, I'd taken too long to figure it out because he was grabbing me by the waist and lifting me from the counter before spinning me around. "Grab on."

I gripped the edge of the counter as Damien sank down behind me, his hot lips pressing against one of my asscheeks before his teeth bit down, and I yelped. He ran his tongue over the mark he'd before going to the other cheek and doing the same thing. Then, when I was sufficiently branded, he spread my ass open, and I struggled to pull free from his grip before his tongue ran over my forbidden hole.

"Stop it," I wiggled against him, but he gripped my hips hard enough to bruise and flicked his tongue against me.

"I'll stop when I'm finished." This time my body felt like it was melting back against him. It was so wrong, but it felt so good how he was taking control of my body to give me pleasure.

I was rewarded for giving in to him as two of his fingers slipped inside of me, pumping so slowly I began to ride them, chasing my next release. Damien pulled his head back, and his fingers left my pussy before he swatted me on the ass. "Hold still."

I whimpered, my grip tightening on the ledge of the counter as he tugged my hips back to him and began to eat my pussy from behind.

"Fuck, you taste so sweet, princess," he groaned against my slit as he licked me teasingly.

"I'm so close," I wined.

"If you want to finish, all you have to do is beg me."

"What?" I snapped, looking back at him over my shoulder. "I don't beg for *anything*."

He jerked my hips turning me to face him. I leaned back against the counter as his mouth latched onto my clit. I threaded my fingers in his hair, watching him suck on me as his eyes smoldered.

"Just like that," I moaned, pushing against his mouth. My legs began to shake, and just as I was about to tumble over the edge, his mouth was no longer on my pussy, and he wore a devilish smirk. "This is torture."

"This is a *lesson*." He corrected me. "You're gonna learn that your pleasure comes from me. No more naughty little shows like you did when I had my friend here, or I'll have to call your mother and let her know that you aren't behaving. If you want to cum, just ask me nicely, and if I feel like you've been a good girl, I'll let you ride my face."

I scowled at him, my hands snaking between my legs as I began to rub my clit, desperate to finish. Damien pushed to his full height, towering over me. He stepped closed, leaving no space between us. His mouth hovered over mine, and I licked my lips, wanting to push up on my toes and kiss him.

"Stop," he ordered.

"Why should I?" I asked, eyebrow cocked in a challenge.

"Because if you don't, I won't give you this." He grabbed my hand from between my legs and placed it over his massive cock rock hard beneath his jeans.

"What makes you think I want it?"

He glanced down between us to where my hand still covered his crotch. His hand was no longer holding it there. I yanked back from him, crossing my arms, which pushed my tits up toward him. He used the back of his finger to lightly trace over the swell of my left breast, and my nipples immediately hardened for him.

"You don't have to be scared. I'll make sure to be extra gentle with your sweet little cunt."

His words made my clit throb. I began to rub myself again, my eyes locked onto his in a challenge. He shook his head like he was disappointed, but he didn't back away, and he held my stare as I came undone. The sound that came from my mouth should have embarrassed me, but I couldn't help myself.

My excitement dripped out of me. Damien grabbed my wrist and raised my hand to his mouth and sucking my fingers clean. His eyes closed momentarily as if savoring the flavor before they snapped back to mine.

"Bad girl." He turned and walked away, leaving me standing naked in the middle of the kitchen.

EIGHT

DAMIEN

My cock was so hard I couldn't think straight, but Valerie was acting like a brat. I knew she wanted me inside of her, but my size could be intimidating, especially to someone as small as she was.

I knew it would take some time to make her feel comfortable, and I was willing to wait. But, we didn't have much time. When her mother came back with my father by her side, she would realize she's been riding her stepbrother's face. I tried to turn her down when she was in her bath, but she practically begged me to fuck her. I was only a man. The look on her face when she saw the size of my cock did something wicked to me. That prissy little attitude made me want something else from her —revenge. Valerie gave me just the ammunition I needed when she admitted that she didn't want her mother to know she was here.

I wanted more than anything to go back in that kitchen and lick her clean, but she disobeyed my orders. I couldn't reward a spoiled little brat. Although it was cute how she used fingering herself to somehow get back at me when there was nothing more beautiful than watching her get off when she was thinking of me.

I didn't even bother closing the door to my bedroom as I stripped off my clothing and laid down on my bed. I began to jerk my cock like a horny fucking teenager as another stupid fucking song began to blare over the speakers. I did my best to ignore the mind-numbing noise. All I could taste and smell was Valerie's pussy.

I closed my eyes, picturing her pink little cunt dripping for me as I began to move my fist faster. That's when I heard a floorboard creak, and I looked over, catching a glimpse of Valerie. She sank back into the darkness of the hallway, and I laid back on the pillow, pretending I hadn't seen her. If she wanted to watch, I would let her. I wasn't shy by any means.

I knew she wished I was fucking her right now. I was glad she was watching me choose to cum by my own hand rather than inside of her. But that didn't mean knowing she was watching didn't make my cock even harder.

She probably had her fingers pressed against her clit right now. "Fuck," I groaned as my cum shot out of me in hot sticky ropes, coating my stomach. I pushed from the bed and headed into my bathroom to take a much-needed hot shower.

NINE

VALERIE

Watching Damien get his dick sucked by some girl was hot. I could admit that. But watching him jerk off was something else entirely. I'd never seen so much cum in my life. The way his muscles flexed and pulled as he stroked himself made my clit pulse with need.

But I wasn't about to go help him out. I was still mad he didn't finish getting me off. I knew I deserved for him to get me worked up and walk away after doing the same to him in the tub, but that didn't make me any less frustrated.

After watching my own little personal porn show starring Damien and his cock, I trudged to my bedroom and collapsed on my bed, exhausted.

***

I awoke a few hours later, the house pitch black. A noise outside of my window had startled me awake, and I lay frozen in fear as I stared over at my curtain. I couldn't see if anything was out there on my balcony.

Finally, after not moving or even breathing for what felt like an eternity, I slid off my bed and went running down the hall to Damien's room in only a tank top and panties.

I banged against the wood, fear consuming me. The door yanked open, and Damien stood on the other side in nothing but black boxer briefs as he rubbed his palm against his eye.

"Something is outside my room." My words came out in a rushed whisper. That woke him right up, and he stepped out between me and the rest of the house.

"Go in my room, princess. I'll be right back."

I bit my lip, nodding. I didn't even argue that he had called me princess. I slipped inside his personal space, crawling into the center of his bed and pulling the covers up to my face, which was a mistake because they smelled just like him.

After a couple of minutes, Damien was back, looking much more relaxed. "It's nothing. A tree branch was hitting the railing."

"Oh. Okay." I began to push up from the bed. "Are you sure? Did you check if the balcony door was locked?"

"I did. I even inspected your closet and bathroom. You're safe. I'm more dangerous than anything out there. Trust me." His lips quirked up in a cocky smirk.

"Okay." But I didn't move. I couldn't. When I was sixteen, our house was robbed while I was sleeping. Of course, now we had the best alarm money could buy, but that didn't take away the fear of knowing someone had been in your room while you were in there, none the wiser.

"Do you want to sleep with me, princess?" he asked.

"Yes," I whispered, not even caring about the double meaning behind his words.

"Just so you know." He grabbed his underwear and shoved them down to his feet before kicking them off. "I sleep naked. I only put those on because I didn't know who was banging on my door.

I slid over to the edge of the bed, but even Damien's naked body couldn't scare me back to my room. I rolled onto my side, away from him, and pulled the cover around me as I felt his side of the bed dip.

I felt safer here, but I couldn't seem to get my breathing under control, and Damien noticed. His large hand gripped my arm, rolling me onto my back as he looked down at me with a furrowed brow.

"You really are scared. I thought you made that who thing up to get into my bed."

I glared at him, causing him to chuckle. "We had someone break in here once," I confessed.

"And you came back here thinking you were gonna stay alone?" he asked.

"I didn't really have a choice. After Chase..." I broke away from his gaze, hating that I even brought my ex up.

"After Chase *what*? Finish that sentence, princess. If you tell me he hurt you, I'll go make sure to break every one of his fingers so he can't lay them on you again."

"No, it wasn't that. He... he cheated on me."

Damien wrapped his arms around me, crushing me to his muscular chest. I snuggled into his hold, and for the first time since I'd caught Chase, I broke down and cried. Damien held me through each shudder until finally, I was too tired to care anymore, and I passed out in his arms.

TEN

DAMIEN

I held Valerie the entire night. I didn't know who that prick Chase was, but he was an absolute fucking idiot for letting someone like her go. Yeah, she was a brat, and my dick was perpetually hard around her, but she didn't deserve to be hurt that way.

Light poured through my window, and I had to get up, but I didn't want to wake her. I knew she probably indulged in a little too much alcohol last night and could use the extra sleep. But if I didn't get this raging hard-on taken care of soon, I was going to explode.

I rolled to my back, and Valerie curled into my side with her head propped on my arm like a pillow. It felt good having her tight little body against me. I wasn't used to it. I'd fucked my fair share of women, but they always left when we finished. I liked my personal space to be mine. But there was no way I could tell Valerie no last night when she looked so scared. And I'd be lying if I said I didn't enjoy having my dick nestled up against her plump ass.

I grabbed my length with my free hand and slowly began to work my grip up and down, trying not to shake the bed. Valerie stirred, her warm palm splaying over my stomach, and she made a needy little noise that caused my cock to swell even thicker.

I slowly began to work my shaft again, thinking about her tight little pussy and how good it would feel to be inside of her when I realized her breathing had changed, no longer deep and even. Now her breathes came out in shallow pants like she was turned on. She was awake, but she didn't move, and she was watching me.

I continued to stroke my cock, groaning as I ran my thumb over the sensitive head. "You want to help me, princess? I promise to return the favor."

She gasped when she realized she'd been caught. I took her hand from my stomach and wrapped her fingers around my dick, underneath mine, guiding her up and down my length. I hissed between my teeth because it felt so fucking good. I was going to cum hard and fast. "Just like that," I rasped into her hair. Her fingers flexed around me. She liked being praised. I let my hand fall to the side so I could watch her jerk me off. After a few more pumps, my stomach muscles tightened, and I came all over her hand.

I grabbed my shirt from yesterday and wiped her hand and my stomach clean. "Now it's my turn."

I crawled over her, and she fell onto her back, her legs already splayed, exposing a wet spot in the middle of her cotton panties. She was already dripping for me.

"What is it you want, princess? My fingers, my mouth, or my cock?"

Her teeth sank into her plump lower lip, her eyes at half-mast. "Mouth, please."

My cock jerked at her use of the word *please*, and I couldn't help but smile as I sank between her legs, placing a kiss against her pussy over top of her panties.

Sliding the fabric to the side, I delved into her with my tongue. I couldn't get enough of her taste and her smell. Valerie's fingers tangled in my hair, tugging at it to pull me closer. I smiled against her skin, licking her slowly and taking my time.

Spreading her open, I flicked my tongue over her clit, and she cried out, grinding back against my mouth with a needy whimper. The sounds she made caused my cock to thicken.

"Fuck," I whispered, wrapping my fingers around her panties and tugging them roughly. The fabric bit into her skin before giving way and falling loose around her hip. I slid them off her spread her back open, needing to be buried between her thighs. "The things I would do to this pussy," I groaned.

I was rewarded with a low moan as Valerie's legs started to tremble. I rubbed against her clit, licking her clean as she came against my mouth.

Crawling up over her body, I let my thick cock fall between her legs, rubbing against her as I pushed her tank top over her tits so I could suck a nipple into my mouth. "Take this off," I ordered as I climbed off the bed.

"Why?" she asked as she sat up and tugged it over her head. I liked that she was much better at listening today after I protected her last night and held her in my arms. But I also enjoyed her feisty side because punishing her made me hard. I let my eyes skate down over her body before turning away from her and walking toward my bathroom. "I want to clean you up so I can make you dirty again."

"I already got what I wanted from you," she snapped. There was my little brat.

I smiled before glancing over my shoulder at her just as she pushed from my bed and sauntered out of the room completely nude.

I didn't chase her like I knew she wanted. Instead, I hopped in the shower and jerked my cock to the thought of fucking her.

ELEVEN

VALERIE

Being woken by Damien stroking his massive cock made me instantly slick between my legs. I knew if I played his little game and asked nicely, I could get him to go down on me again. But that didn't make us friends. Far from it. Still, I was grateful he was there when I thought someone was going to break into the house last night. I only wished I'd never mentioned Chase. He didn't need to know any of the shitty details of my life that brought me here. At least, for the few days I had to put up with him, I could use him for what I needed.

I sauntered down the kitchen, grabbing a peach from the fridge and took a bite before wiping the juice from my chin. Damien came downstairs right after I sank down on the couch, his eyes roaming over me before stopping at the fruit in my hand. I tried to hide my disappointment that he was now wearing jeans slung low on his hips.

"You have a bad habit of eating things that aren't yours," he bit out.

"I could say the same to you," I retorted, taking another bite and moaning at how good it tasted.

His eyes narrowed as he walked closer to me.

"Want a taste?" I asked.

He nodded, his tongue running out over his lower lip. I held it out to him, but he leaned down over me, capturing my lower lip between his and sucking on it. My cunt instantly clenched, and I let my mouth fall open, granting him access. His tongue slid against mine, and he kissed me just like he had between my legs.

When he pulled back from me, I rubbed the juicy fruit over my nipple, causing it to bud. Damien growled, bending lower and sucking it into his mouth and lapping the sticky juices from my skin. I slid my hand down further, spreading my thighs wide as I rubbed it against my clit. I was so sensitive and desperate for his touch. I ground my hips against the peach, moaning as the nectar coated me. Damien sank to his knees and began to clean up the mess with his tongue, licking against my folds as I continued to grind against the peach.

I came so fast, and hard I saw flashes of light. But he didn't let up, continuing to lap at me until my hand fell to my thigh, entirely spent.

Damien grabbed the peach from my hand and took a bite from it, moaning as if it was the best thing he'd ever tasted. "Thanks for breakfast," he muttered with a wink before turning and walking out of the room.

He hadn't even hinted at having sex with me, leaving me wondering what his angle was. He'd given me exactly what I wanted, and I didn't need to beg, but now I was left feeling like I had played right into his hand.

****

After a quick shower, I went out to lay by the pool as I played on my phone. Damien had disappeared for a few hours, and I actually missed having him around. When I wasn't getting off or picking a fight with him, I was left to think about Chase. I just wanted to forget that he ever existed, which was hard to do when he continued to text me, begging for me to take him back.

TWELVE

DAMIEN

I knew Valerie got off on teasing me, but she had no self-control. So after getting herself all worked up, I got to bury my face between her thighs and eat her out. But nothing prepared me for how hot it was to watch her fuck a peach as I licked the juices from her cunt.

I'd gone down on her more times than I could count. I was becoming addicted to her taste, and if I wasn't careful, she would catch feelings. That's why I usually didn't fuck a girl more than once. But technically, we hadn't done the deed yet, and I was still desperate to feel her pussy clench down on me and milk my cock. I couldn't help myself.

I decided going for a run was exactly what I needed. Without PT every day, I had to do something to keep myself in shape and clear my head.

***

I slipped back into the house, soaked in sweat with my t-shirt thrown over my shoulder as I pulled open the fridge to grab a bottle of water. When I closed it, Valerie was standing on the other side of the door with her arms crossed over her chest.

"Where were you?" She asked.

I smirked, shaking my head. "None of your business, princess."

"I thought something happened to you."

That comment made me feel like shit. I thought she was being a nosey little brat, but she was actually worried about me. Still, I didn't need her caring about me, and this was a step too close. I had to put up some boundaries. I would be leaving this place in my rearview soon, and I wasn't the type to get attached. With my line of work, it was better not to have someone left behind to cry about you while you were in the sandbox. And worrying about them while you're getting shot at was dangerous.

"I can handle myself," I replied, downing the rest of my water before turning and walking upstairs to take a shower.

I stayed in my room for a couple of hours, watching a movie, until crappy pop music began to blare over the house speakers.

I hit pause on the television and stomped down the steps to find Valerie dancing in her panties and bra with a bottle of liquor in her hand. I clicked off the music, causing her to spin around to look at me, sloshing alcohol onto the floor.

"Hey, I was dancing to that."

"Are you... even old enough to drink that?" I asked, stepping closer to her. My fingers wrapped around the bottle, and she let it go without a fight.

"Little late to be asking that," she shot back, unable to wipe the goofy smile from her face. "I'm already drunk."

"I can see that." I took a swig of the harsh liquid as I watched her continue to move her hips to the imaginary music.

"I'll be twenty-one in two years," she slurred as if saying it that way made her sound older.

"If your liver makes it that long," I quipped. Valerie let out an unladylike snort before breaking into a fit of giggles. "Are you really only nineteen?" I asked, and she nodded with a grin.

"How old are you?" she asked, her finger dancing over her flat stomach as she pressed her teeth into her lower lip.

"Old enough to know better," I groaned, taking another drink as my eyes danced over her. "I'm twenty-six." Admitting my age makes me feel dirty. I shouldn't be trying to dip my cock in someone so young, someone who had no idea she's my family now. I took another drink. I wouldn't be able to just walk away from her. She'd be at family events, and I'd have to see her during the holidays. I hadn't thought any of this through. Still, my cock stood to attention as she let her finger sink lower, tracing the edge of her tiny white panties.

"I think maybe you should lay down."

Valerie's cheeks darkened. "With you?"

I ran my tongue out over my lower lip at the thought of tasting her again, but I shook my head no. "Playtime is over, princess. And I have a friend coming over later."

"A *friend*?" she asked, unable to hide the hurt from her eyes. *Shit.* I knew that look. I'd seen it before, right before I walked away and out of a woman's life for good. That's why I tried to stay away from women who weren't my age. They got clingy fast.

"She'll be here soon, and I plan to fuck her on that couch," I motioned to the spot where I'd eaten her peachy pussy. Her gaze followed mine before looking back at me with narrowed eyes.

"You're serious?" she asked.

"You're welcome to watch again. You seemed to really enjoy it last time," I shot back with a wink. This was the moment I usually got slapped, but Valerie just narrowed her eyes like she was trying to figure out what game I was playing.

"That's fine," she replied with a shrug, taking the bottle from my hand and tipping it to her lips before handing it back to me.

"Really?" I asked, watching her as she walked over to the fridge, pulling it open like she was studying the contents.

Grabbing a peach, she took a large bite and didn't even bother wiping away the juice that dripped down her chin. I wanted desperately to lick her clean, but instead, I chugged another sip of the whiskey.

"I'm going out anyway."

I shook my head, grinning sardonically. "No, you're not."

"Excuse me?"

THIRTEEN

VALERIE

I didn't know who the hell Damien thought he was, but he wasn't going to tell me what to do. Standing in front of him and pretending it didn't piss me off that he was bringing over some random stranger to fuck while we had been messing around was nearly impossible. Not that it wasn't scorching the way he watched me while getting his dick sucked by what's her name. But I didn't like to share. I was thankful for the alcohol that warmed my veins and helped dull the ache he'd caused in my chest because I wanted him to want me. I'd enjoyed teasing him.

Two could play these games, and I was much better at it. I learned to be a spoiled vindictive bitch from the best there was, my mother.

"You heard me. You're drunk. Sit that pretty little ass down. You aren't going anywhere."

"It's not up to you."

"Really?" he asked before taking another drink. "Who is it up to then? Your mother? Should I give her a call?" My eyes narrowed as I folded my arms across my chest.

"I'm an adult," I snapped.

"Hardly. And you aren't old enough to be completely wasted, so you aren't going anywhere unless you want to get arrested."

"I'm going."

"You have to the count of three to go up to bed before I make you."

I rolled my eyes, taking another bite of my peach as I leaned my elbows on the island.

"One."

I sighed, licking the juice from my lower lip.

"Two."

I narrowed my eyes at him in a challenge.

"Don't say I didn't warn you." Sitting the bottle down on the counter, he pushed from his stool and walked up behind me. I yelped, dropping my peach on the ground as he spun me around and hoisted me up over his shoulder. My ass was next to his face, and he slapped it, causing me to squeal as we made our way up the stairs and down the hallway. To my surprise, we walked right by my bedroom and turned into his, dropping me onto his bed. His eyes smoldered as he looked down at me. "Three."

"You can't do this." I pushed up on my elbows.

"You're lucky this is *all* I'm doing to you right now."

"What is that supposed to mean?"

He leaned down over me with a hand on either side of my waist, so his hot breath blew across my lips. "It means I don't think you can handle the way I really want to punish you, so you're getting off easy."

I snorted out a laugh. "*Getting off easy* is what you should call your date," I made air quotes with my fingers. His eyes narrowed.

My laughter died in my throat as he loomed over me, the muscles in his jaw jumping under his taut skin before he undid his pants and shoved them down, leaving him straining against his black boxer briefs. "You have two choices, princess. You can either stay in my bed like a good little girl, or I can tie you to it."

"Go to hell," I spit back at him.

Damien shrugged, seemingly unphased by my reaction, as he turned and pulled open the drawer of his nightstand and grabbing a pair of black handcuffs. "You can fight me if you want. But, I'm going to be honest, I'll enjoy it more if you struggle." He punctuated that comment with a wink. I groaned, raising my hands above my head.

Damien crawled over me, a knee on either side of my waist as he leaned forward and fastened the cuffs through a slat of the headboard. I raised my hips, pushing myself against his groin. He groaned, grabbing me and shoving me back against the bed as he shook his head.

"You need a time out," he said with a smirk before climbing off the bed and padding his way to his bathroom. A few seconds later, I heard the water of his shower turn on.

FOURTEEN

DAMIEN

If Valerie wasn't drunk, I would have given her a third option, let me fuck her until her cunt was milking my cock. But I didn't want her to do something that she might regret. And the goal of all of this was to make sure she understood that whatever happened between us was over.

I quickly washed myself up, my cock painfully hard. I shouldn't have brought Valerie to my bed, but in the heat of the moment, I wanted nothing more than to rip her panties off and spank her until she came.

I dried myself off and walked back into my bedroom, surprised Valerie wasn't struggling to free herself from her restraints. Instead, she watched me, her eyes trained on my hard cock.

"What are you doing, princess?" I asked, taking a few steps closer. "See something you want?"

"You wish."

"Keep telling yourself that," I replied dryly as I stepped into my closet and got dressed. "Well, this has been fun, but my friend should be here soon." With that, I left my room and hurried downstairs as Valerie screamed obscenities. I turned on the sound system and cranked her shitty music to drown her out before sinking down on the couch and watching a movie. My dick was hard enough to crack granite, and I wished I really did having some random hookup coming over to fuck. I'd only said that because Valerie looked at me like she wanted to swallow my cock whole, and I need to put some space between us.

***

After my horror movie ended, a slasher flick with bouncing tits and lots of blood, I decided it was time to go to bed. But, unfortunately, that's where'd I'd left Valerie. I hoped she was passed out and slept off some of her inebriation, so maybe she would stop acting like a fucking brat.

I turned off the music and all the lights before trudging up the stairs. Valerie was still in the center of my bed, blinking her eyes open at the sound of me coming in. *Fuck*, she looked so hot tied up and waiting for me in her panties and bra. My dick went rock hard at the sight of her.

I pulled my t-shirt over my head and tossed it on the floor before shoving my jeans down and kicking them off. I palmed my cock over my underwear.

"My arms hurt."

"Your lucky it isn't your ass that hurts," I quipped, earning me a glare. Crawling over her, I undid the cuffs, rubbing her wrists gently before looking down at her below me. I rubbed my cock again as her tongue ran out over her lips.

"Your *friend* didn't take care of that?" she asked. "I could help you out," she offered, cocking an eyebrow. I thought of pulling myself out and rubbing my dick against her pink lips. "*If* you take care of me first."

"I'm not falling for that." I laughed as I climbed off her and laid down, turning on my side toward her and grabbing her, tugging her so her back was against my chest and my cock pushed up against her ass.

FIFTEEN

VALERIE

I wiggled my ass back against Damien's dick, causing him to groan as his arm banded tighter around me. His mouth was at my ear. "Don't tempt me, princess."

A shiver rolled through me, and he chuckled.

"How was your date?" I snapped.

He groaned, rubbing his dick against me. "Her cunt was so wet and tight."

"Fuck you," I swung my elbow back, hitting him in the ribs. That earned me a laugh as he rolled onto his back, and I immediately missed his hold on me.

"I didn't have a date," he confessed. I turned over to face him and his eyes connected to mine with no hint of amusement. He was telling the truth.

"She canceled?"

He shrugged, closing his eyes like I was boring him into sleep. "I lied." He cracked an eye open to look at me. "Because this," he motioned between us, "is a bad idea. And the sooner we both understand that, the better."

I rolled my eyes. "I don't want you anyway."

"So your pussy isn't dripping right now?" he asked.

"So your cock is rock hard right now?" I shot back, earning me another devastation grin.

"Go to sleep, princess."

I rolled on my back, staring up at the ceiling. There was no way this asshole kept me tied to the bed for God knows how long, and now he wasn't even going to make me cum. I slipped my hand into my panties and began to rub my clit. After a few minutes, a whimper escaped me. I usually could make myself cum within seconds, but now, my body was getting used to having Damien's mouth on me. And that's all I wanted. It felt so good the way his stubble rubbed against my sensitive, smooth flesh.

"Stop petting your kitty," Damien growled.

"I need to get off," I whined, rubbing faster. I watched as his hand slid down over his abs and gripped his cock over his underwear, illuminated by the moonlight that poured through his window.

I slid my bra down and unhooked it before tossing it on the floor, palming one of my tits as I continued to rub myself.

"Then take off your panties so I can watch you," Damien ordered. I quickly slid them down, and he did the same, stroking his length as I slipped my hand back between my legs. "Finger yourself."

"I want you to go down on me," I begged, but he only shook his head.

"I told you, this needs to stop."

I slipped a finger inside of myself. I was soaking wet.

"Tell me how it feels."

"It feels…" I panted, "so good." I licked my lips, watching as he jacked himself off. "Let me ride you."

"What?"

"Not with you… inside of me. Just let me rub myself against you." I pushed up on my knees, still rubbing my clit as I waited for him to agree. "Please," I begged, reaching out to rub my hand over the head of his cock with my wet fingers. He drug his teeth over his lower lip, and that move alone nearly made me cum.

"I love it when you beg, princess."

I slid my leg over Damien's waist and pressed my clit against his cock. His hands found my hips, gripping me tight enough to bruise as I rolled forward. Embarrassment heated my cheeks, and I stilled.

"What?" He asked.

"I...um... don't know how to do it."

The look in his eyes changed from turned on to looking like he wanted to devour me. "Are you a virgin?" he asked, pushing up on one of his elbows.

I nodded, covering my face with my hands.

"And you were going to let me fuck you in that tub without saying anything?"

I nodded again. "I just got scared. But we could try..." Damien grabbed my wrist and pulled my arm down before laying on his back and grabbing my hips again. He tugged me forward and rocked me back slowly, causing pleasure to shoot up through my belly.

"Just like that, sweetheart. Just rub that sweet little cunt against me." I pressed my hands against his chest, moving with his hands as he rolled my hips.

"You're so fucking beautiful," he whispered, and I felt my pussy clench, desperate to have him inside of me. "You're gonna make me cum."

Those words sent me over the edge, and pleasure rippled through my body, drenching Damien's cock in my juices. His grip on me tightened, and he dragged me back over his length a final time before his cum shot out between us all over his stomach.

With a ragged breath, he grabbed my arms and pulled my body down against him, and wrapped his arms around me. He held me like that until my body stopped shaking before grabbing a washrag and cleaning us both up.

***

SIXTEEN

DAMIEN

The moment I woke up, my head was throbbing from the alcohol I'd consumed. My eyes when to Valerie, who was still fast asleep beside me. Visions of her rubbing herself against my cock assaulted me, and I felt like I was going to be sick. It was bad enough I was keeping the fact that I was her stepbrother from her. But finding out she was a virgin, and I nearly deflowered her within minutes of meeting her, made me sick.

I wasn't deserving of that gift. And it wouldn't be long until she figured out who I really was. I pushed from the bed and began to gather my things, shoving them into my green duffle bag.

"What are you doing?"

I stood to my full height and turned to see Valerie sitting up, the sheet from my bed bunched around her waist, exposing her perky tits.

I shook my head and went back to shoving my clothing in the bag, wishing I'd put on more than my underwear to conceal how hard she makes me. "I have to go back to the base."

"What? *Now*?"

I closed my eyes, cursing myself in my head.

"Is this because..." her voice cracked. "Because of what I told you?"

I turned back around to look at her. She'd pulled the sheet up under her chin and was looking at me like I'd just ripped out her heart. I wanted to go to her and wrap my arms around her and tell her that her being a virgin wasn't something she should ever be ashamed of. But I wasn't deserving of that gift. As far as I was concerned, no one deserved her. "No, princess." I dropped my bag, trying and failing to convince myself that I was doing the right thing. "But I can't be the one to take that from you."

"You wouldn't be taking it. I'd be giving it –"

"*No*, Valerie," I barked. I hung my head, running my fingers through my hair as I exhaled. I sank down on the edge of the bed, my elbows on my knees as I hung my head.

Valerie placed her hand on my back before pulling away. "What did I do wrong?" She sounded so young, so vulnerable.

"I need to tell you something." I turned to look at her. "And I need you not to freak out."

"Okay," she drew out the words as she pulled her knees to her chest and wrapped her arms around them to hug herself, putting her little pussy on display for me.

I swallowed back the bile rising in my throat. "I uh…" I rubbed my hand over the back of my neck before shaking my head. I couldn't say it. Not when she was looking at me like that with her lower lip caught between her teeth. I squeezed my eyes closed. "I never properly introduced myself to you."

I glanced over at her, I couldn't help myself, and I was rewarded with her cheeks darkening, and I could see her pussy was glistening. "My name is Damien Wentworth."

Her eyes narrowed as she thought about what I'd just told her. "Wentworth? As in –"

"As in Roland Wentworth, your mother's new husband."

"You're... *You're* my *stepbrother*?"

I swallowed hard, reaching out to her, but she scooted back on the bed out of reach. "You... you... asshole," she yelled, causing me to chuckle as she pushed from the bed and searched for her bra and panties.

"I never denied being an asshole," I replied.

"This isn't funny."

I bit back a snarky comment because she was right. It was seriously fucked up, and even now, I couldn't stop thinking about sinking my cock inside of her.

I grabbed her wrist as she passed in front of me, tugging her toward me.

"I'm sorry, princess."

She tugged against my grip as her eyes searched mine.

"I should have told you right away, but you begged me to touch you, and I couldn't help myself." I pulled her closer and pressed my lips against her stomach. I felt her body sway toward mine.

"This is so wrong," she whispered. "But it feels *so* fucking good," I groaned. I pressed my lips against her again, and her eyes fell closed as she let out a little sigh. I dipped lower, licking her cunt as my arms looped around her and pulled her harder against me. "I needed to taste you." I sucked her clit into my mouth while curling my hand under her left knee and raising it to prop on the bed next to me so I could get better access. Her fingers slid into my hair, tugging my face against her as she ground against me, whimpering.

SEVENTEEN

VALERIE

I was livid and confused but completely turned on. I rocked my hips against Damien's mouth, fucking his tongue as I gripped his hair, tugging on him enough to cause him to groan. But he didn't let up.

"I don't know if I can forgive you."

"Tell me what I can do. If you want me to leave now, I will."

I chewed my lip, my body begging for more. "I...I want you to deflower me."

"Princess..."

"Please? I want to know what it feels like. I want you to make me feel good," I begged.

He grabbed my hips, lifting me and flipping me onto my back in the center of the bed before crawling over me as he shoved down his boxer briefs to free his cock. He grabbed the base of his length in his hand as he rubbed his head against my clit.

His tongue forced its way into my mouth, and I could taste my excitement on him. "I can't get enough of you," he confessed against my lips. I rolled my hips, my body shaking. "Tell me to stop."

I shook my head, desperate for my release, as he kicked his underwear completely off.

"Tell me to stop touching your pussy, princess," he whispered against my neck as he nipped and sucked my flesh. I rolled my head to the side, granting him access.

"Please fuck me." I snaked my hand down between us, circling my fingers over his, and pushed him lower, so the head of his dick was against my entrance. He thrust forward, letting just the tip of him slip inside of me. My back bowed off the bed as I rubbed against my slick nub.

"You're too fucking tight, sweetheart. I don't want to hurt you."

"Already playing the protective big brother?" I whimpered again, pushing back against him. "You already hurt me when you lied to me," I whispered before pushing down again, crying out as he slipped another inch inside of me.

"Let me kiss it and make it better, little sister." He groaned as he threw my words back at me from the first night in the tub. His mouth latched around my nipple, and he sucked it hard, pulling it into a peak before doing the same to the other. Then, without warning, he thrust forward, and I screamed as he seated himself entirely inside of me. He didn't move, allowing me to adjust to the violent intrusion as he continued to lap against my skin. My pussy burned, and it felt like he was going to rip me in two.

"Shhh... I promise I'll make it feel good again, baby," he whispered in my ear as he reached between us and pushed against my clit. I mewled, and I felt his lips turn up in a smile against my neck. "I'm gonna fuck you now," he warned, drawing back slowly and rocking his hips back forward. My body was tense, afraid of the pain that was to come, but as he continued to roll his hips, the burn began to ebb, and left behind was a delicious feeling of being completely filled. "That's my good little girl," he cooed. "Take me all the way in your sweet little cunt." He thrust forward a little harder now, his heavy balls slapping against my ass.

"What if our parents come home? They could catch us," I warned, worried about how wanton and reckless we were being.

"I'm not stopping until I fill you up," He warned as he lifted his weight from my body, and I immediately regretted my stupid question. But Damien didn't pull out of me, only sat up on his knees and gripped my hips so he could hold me still and fuck me. His eyes settled on the way my tits bounced with each thrust of his cock. "I think they'd be happy we play so well together," he quipped, moving a little faster and causing me to moan. His thumb found my clit, and he licked his lips as he rubbed against me, looking like he was torn between wanting to keep fucking me and eating me out.

I let my eyes fall closed as pleasure began to build in my belly.

"That's it, princess. Milk my cock and fill that pretty little cunt with my seed."

His words sent me tumbling over the edge, and I felt my pussy grip down on his length as he swelled impossibly hard inside of me. Then, he began to fuck me hard, pumping in and out of me as his cum filled me, running out of my hole with each thrust and dripping down my ass.

He groaned as he pulled his still semi-hard cock from me, and I winced as I noticed the blood smeared on his skin. He reached out, running his finger along my slit. "Fuck, that was so hot, princess. Look how pretty your pussy is when it's dripping with my cum." He climbed off the bed before bending down and pressing a soft kiss to my clit.

"I can't believe we just did that," I said in a daze, propping myself up on my elbows.

"I'm not done breaking you in yet, little sis."

EIGHTEEN

DAMIEN

I slid my arms under her and lifted her against my chest to carry her to my bathroom. I sat her down on wobbly legs, making sure she was steady before turning on the faucet in the tub.

"What are you doing?" she asked, looking like she could use a nap.

"I'm going to scrub you clean, and then I am going to take my time making you filthy again."

***

After scrubbing every inch of Valerie's body, including her pink and swollen cunt until she came again, I dried her off and carried her back to my bed, spreading her naked body out of the covers. My cock was already throbbing, desperate to be inside of her again, but I knew I needed to give her time to recover.

Instead, I crawled over her, licking her clit on my way up her body before laying down beside her and jerking my dick in my hand.

"It's time for your breakfast, little sis. I want to cum in every one of your holes." I grinned at the way her cheeks darkened at my dirty words. She sat up, stretching with a yawn. Poor little thing was exhausted from our fuck session. I'd have to let her rest as soon as she finished sucking me off.

"It's so big," she whined as she watched me stroke my length, licking her lips. I loved how she pretended to be so innocent.

"I know, princess. And it's waiting for you to make it happy." I tangled my fingers in her hair and guided her head down to my waist. "Suck on it like I told you to or I'll have to call your mom and tell her your misbehaving."

"No. I'll be a good girl, I promise." She slid her tongue over the head of my cock, eliciting a groan from the back of my throat. The sound spurred her own, and she wrapped her lips around my head, sucking hard and making a popping sound as it sprang free from her lips. "Mmm... do that again."

She took my head into her mouth again, and I pushed my hips up, sinking deeper into her mouth. "Take it deeper. Let it hit the back of your throat. I want to make you gag."

She worked her way lower, bobbing up and down several times before finally letting it touch the back of her throat.

"Fuck," I groaned, my balls drawing up. "Put your leg over me so I can eat that tight little cunt while you swallow my cock."

"Damien," she whimpered, and I jerked my dick a few times, loving how she whined when she was scared of what my thick shaft could do to her. "Don't make me ask you again, princess."

Valerie threw her leg over me and leaned back so her pretty little cunt, still swollen and red from my violation, was directly above my mouth. I swiped my tongue against her slit, and she bucked before latching on to my dick and sucking with vigor. Dragged my finger over her slick folds, I rubbed her juices up over her asshole. She pulled away and released my dick, and I grabbed her hips, forcing her to sit on my face as I began to eat her out. When she was rubbing her kitty against my face, making the sexiest fucking noises I'd ever heard, I moved my tongue to her ass and began to lick over her back door.

"Take my cock back in your mouth, or I'm putting it here," I warned, punctuating my statement by pressing my tongue into her ass. She grabbed my dick, sucking it back until it made her gag again as she worked the rest of the length in her fist."

I slipped a finger inside of her pussy, and she began to ride it, her walls gripping down and sucking my digit deeper inside of her. "Damn, baby, look how greedy your cunt is."

She moaned, and my cock thickened against her tongue. I began to buck my hips upward, fucking her mouth, and I shot my load back her throat. Her creamy cunt coated my face in her juices, and I licked up every last drop she gave me before she was painting on top of me, stroking my cock until it softened.

"Come here, sweetheart." I slapped her ass, causing her to yelp before she turned around and snuggled into my side with her tits pressed against me, and we drifted back off to sleep.

***

NINETEEN

VALERIE

I awoke in my own bed. I pushed up from my pillow, searching my dimly lit room for Damien. *Had I dreamed it all?* The soreness between my legs let me know that what I had done with my stepbrother wasn't a fantasy at all. It was very real. I quickly tugged on my clothing and brushed my teeth before slipping into the hall and down the stairs. I stopped short at the sound of other voices. *My mother. Oh, God.* I forced a smile and continued out to the kitchen, where my eyes locked on Damien's, who wore a wicked grin as he raised a cup of coffee to his lips.

"Hey, princess," my mother called out, and Damien made a choking sound. I forced a smile and walked over to give her a hug, thankful I'd decided to get dressed.

"Hello, mother. I hope you had a good trip."

"Oh, you know how traveling just wears me out," she replied flippantly. "I didn't know you were here, or I would have had a grocery service fill the cupboards for you.”

“Oh, it was no big deal.” My cheeks blushed as I thought of the dirty things we’d done with a peach and how he punished me after I’d eaten his salad.

“Where is Chase? Sleeping in?”

“Oh, um… no. He didn’t come,” I waved her off as I went to the coffee machine and poured myself a mug.

“You came alone?”

That caused Damien to clear his throat, and I glared over at him over the rim of my steaming mug. “Where is your new husband? I thought I would get the chance to meet him,” I lied, not giving a damn about the latest man of the week.

“He is in France doing some work,” she rolled her eyes like she could care less. “I’m sure you’ll get to see him once you finish your out-processing,” she added to Damien.

“Out-processing?” I asked.

“I’m getting out of the Army,” he explained.

"Oh," was all I could say because I was just now realizing how little actual talking we'd done during our naughty time together.

"I'm going to go take a hot bath and relax with a glass of wine. Let's do dinner this evening." My mother called out, not bothering to ask if I already had plans. I didn't. But the last thing I wanted to do was be forced to sit with her and Damien and try not to blush.

Leaning down, she pressed a kiss to my cheek before sauntering off. Once she was out of earshot, I glared at Damien.

"Why didn't you wake me?" I whispered.

"You needed to rest after..." his eyes drug down my body and back to mine. "everything."

I felt my body grow hot, and he glanced down at my nipples that had hardened beneath my tank top. I put my cup on the island, suddenly not in need of caffeine.

"This is bad. This is very, very bad," I warned him, feeling the panic rising in my chest. Damien sat his mug down and walked toward me, and I pressed my palms against his chest, wanting to push him away but unable not to touch him. Instead, he stepped closer until his hips were against mine and brushed my hair from my face, tucking it behind my ear.

"Look at me."

Reluctantly I tilted my chin up to meet his gaze. "How could anything that felt *so fucking good* be bad?" he asked, his eyes smoldering. I swallowed hard as he leaned down and brushed his lips against mine. His mouth went to my ear, and he whispered, "I want to taste you again."

I felt myself grow slick at his dirty words, and I hated how he was able to turn me on whenever he wanted.

"Damien…"

He slid his thumb across my lower lip before dipping it into my mouth. My tongue pressed back against his intrusion, and he groaned. "Are you wet for me, princess?"

I nodded, sucking on his thumb before he pulled it back out of my mouth and traced my jaw.

"Show me?"

"What?" I asked, my eyes flitting to the doorway my mother had exited through.

"Pull your shorts down and show me how wet you are for me."

I slid my shorts down a few inches, just enough to expose my clit. Damien made a hungry noise in the back of his throat as he slid the pad of his finger against me before raising it to his mouth and licking my juices from his skin. "Take them off."

"Are you crazy? We could get caught."

"This," he rubbed his finger against my clit again. "is mine. And I'll do *what* I want with it *when* I want it."

"Please –"

"I love it when you beg me, little sis. But if you are going to ask me not to eat your pretty little cunt until you cum on my tongue, don't bother wasting your breath." He grabbed the front of my shorts, and I rocked my hips forward, grazing my sensitive bud against his knuckles. "Fine. I'm not completely unreasonable." He pulled his thick cock from his shorts and pressed the head against me before slipping between my thighs. His body began to push against mine as he turned me, so my back was against the counter.

"Oh God," I whimpered as he rubbed his length between my folds.

"Shhh... you have to be quiet, or someone is going to catch us," he warned, moving his hips faster. I squeezed my thighs together, and he growled, bucking his hips forward. "I want you to cum on me just like this, and then you can lick me clean." Grabbing my hips, he held me still and began to hump me harder. I let him use me like his own personal fuck toy, enjoying how worked up my body made him. He grabbed my tank top and pulled it up over my tits so he could watch them bounce and sway from his assault. Then, as my legs began to shake and I was panting, he slowed, pulling his cock away from me until only the tip pressed against my clit. "Why didn't you tell your mother that you broke up with Chase?"

"What?" I couldn't wrap my head around his question. I was so lost in the pleasure he'd been giving me.

"Why didn't you tell her that your piece of shit ex cheated on you?"

"Because she wanted me to be with him. She's the one who set us up."

He studied my face for a beat before slowly sliding his cock back between my thighs. I nearly combusted from his touch.

He pushed my shorts down over my ass, his fingers spreading my cheeks apart. "You tell her at dinner or tonight, I'm going to claim this too, and I won't be gentle about it."

I whimpered as his fingertip pressed against my forbidden entrance.

His lips went to my ear. "Unless that's what you want, princess. You want your big brother to ride your ass? You want my cock to stretch out that hole too?"

"No," I panted as he began to thrust forward faster. My hips jutted out to meet his as my cunt started to clench.

"Then you'll be my good little girl and do as I said?"

I nodded my head, biting down on my lip as waves of euphoria rippled through me. Damien watched me come undone as he continued pumping a couple more times before his cum coated my pussy. He took his dick out from between my legs before tugging up my shorts, so his cream smeared all over my lips.

"You can take a bath in an hour. But, right now, I want you walking around with my cum in your panties to remind you who it belongs to. Understood?"

I nodded in a daze.

"Now lick me clean, to show me how much you enjoyed my cock."

I sank to my knees, my eyes locked on his, and ran my tongue over his dick as he watched me approvingly before tucking himself back in his shorts.

I pushed to my feet, gripping the counter behind me.

"We'll finish this later, Sweetheart." He pressed his lips against mine before turning and grabbing his coffee mug, like nothing has happened, and walked out toward the pool.

TWENTY

DAMIEN

The fact that Valerie didn't tell her mother that she wasn't with Chase anymore had my blood boiling. I had to know that just because she'd shown up unexpectantly, what I had with my little princess wasn't over. Even if it meant risking getting caught.

I was losing my fucking mind. The smart thing to do would have been to leave this morning like I had planned, but one look at that pouting face, worried that I wouldn't fuck her, sent me over the edge.

The thought of slipping inside of her virgin cunt bareback made my dick instantly hard. I never fucked anyone without protection, and now I was spilling my seed inside of a girl I had no business fucking, loving the idea that I may make her belly swell from what we did. It was sick.

I was sick.

But I wanted more. I wanted all of her, and her greedy little pussy couldn't get enough of me.

I tilted my head up to the sun, relishing in the warmth. Dinner was going to be awkward and uncomfortable as fuck, but if it meant spending more time with Valerie, I was willing to do almost anything.

***

I kept my distance from everyone for the rest of the day. I wasn't a fan of Pam, and I knew if I stepped foot near her daughter, I'd have to bury myself inside of her. I wanted to keep a clear head. This was my dad's life now, and even if I thought he was chasing after a greedy bitch, that was his decision to make.

All of that came crashing down around me when I heard Pam scream. I hurried down the stairs to find her embracing a man who wasn't my father. When she pulled back to place a palm on either side of his face, I realized he was way too young to be someone interested in her. His face was clean-shaven, his body soft like he'd never done a day's work in his entire life.

"She's going to be so excited to see you, Chase."

My spine stiffened, but I quickly schooled my face and continued toward them.

"Damien, this is Chase, Valerie's fiancé."

That word nearly made me combust. But I forced a smile.

"Hey," he called out to me with a shit-eating grin. "You must be the new big brother." He held out his hand, and I took it, squeezing hard.

"Something like that," I shot back, my eyes going to Valerie's mother.

"Chase?" I heard Valerie call out from behind me, her voice wavering. "What are you doing here?"

Chase looked to Pam, who smirked. "Chase had called me and told me the two of you had a fight," she explained. "So I thought it would be a good idea to invite him over so you can work things out." She winked at her daughter. It wasn't bad enough that Pam was a gold digger. She wanted to make sure her daughter was one as well.

Valerie stepped up beside me, her arms folded across her chest. "I don't have anything to say to him," she snapped.

Pam's face turned severe. "You will act like an adult and talk to Chase, young lady."

Chase took her reprimand as an invitation and walked over to Valerie, pulling her against his chest for a hug. I shoved my hands into my pockets so I wouldn't knock him the hell out.

Valerie pushed against his chest, and he let his hands fall to his sides. "Did you tell my mother *why* we were fighting?"

Chase rubbed over the back of his neck, clearly embarrassed that he was being called out. "Come on, baby," he stepped toward her again, and I put my hand on his chest to force him to keep his distance.

"She made it clear she doesn't want to touch you," I barked in the tone I usually reserved for other soldiers.

Chase glared at me as if his brain couldn't fathom someone telling him no. "*Excuse me?*"

I took a step forward, towering over him. "If you put your hand on her, I'll be putting my hands on *you*. Is that clear enough for you?" I asked.

The column of Chase's throat bobbed as he swallowed hard before looking over his shoulder to Pam.

"Damien –" Pam began to admonish me.

"He cheated on me, mom," Valerie yelled.

Pam looked momentarily taken aback before she began making excuses. "I'm sure there is a reasonable explanation. Did you even give him a chance to explain what happened before throwing one of your tantrums?"

I clenched my jaw. This wasn't my battle to fight, and as much as I wanted to defend Valerie, she had to put her foot down and let them both know precisely what she wanted. I just hoped what she wanted was me.

TWENTY-ONE

VALERIE

I swallowed back the bile rising in my throat. It was one thing to have my mom come home early, but now having my ex standing before me and acting as if he hadn't done anything wrong was driving me crazy.

I was thankful Damien was standing up for me, but if I didn't put an end to this argument now, he may do something that would make it obvious we'd been more intimate than a stepbrother and stepsister should be.

"Look," I paused, choosing my words carefully. "You've both just had long flights, and I'm sure you're tired and hungry. So let's just go to dinner." My shoulders fell, hating that I was giving in, and the broad grin on my mother's face wasn't helping.

Damien looked like he was ready to explode, but he didn't say anything, just turned and made his way back upstairs.

"I should change," I muttered, my eyes going to Chase before I turned and headed to my room.

I slipped inside and pushed the door closed behind me as a hand wrapped around me from behind, covering my mouth to keep me from screaming. Damien's lips were at my ear.

"Don't scream, princess." His hips pushed against my ass, and I could feel how hard he was for me. I nodded, and he released his hold on me so I could turn around to face him. "What the hell was that?" he asked.

"What was I supposed to do? Let things escalate until you hit him?"

"I wouldn't have minded."

"Yeah, well, my mother may have gotten a little suspicious."

Damien took a step closer to me, erasing the space between us. "I'll do whatever you want, sweetheart, but if he puts his hands on you again, I'm going to kill him."

"I don't want him touching me any more than you do."

"Yeah?" Damien asked, a playful glint in his eye. "You want me to touch you, princess?" he asked, pushing his fingers between my legs and rubbing me over my shorts. I let my eyes fall closed, relishing in his touch.

"We can't do this now," I whispered.

"You came to change your clothes, right? Get undressed."

My cheeks began to heat as I grabbed my shirt and tugged it over my head. Damien sank down, sucking one of my nipples into his mouth as he palmed my other breast.

Looping my fingers in my shorts, I shoved them down with my underwear and kicked my clothes off my feet, so I stood completely bare before him. Sinking down on his knees, he latched his mouth onto my pussy and began to suck my clit. I threaded my fingers in his hair, holding him against my mound as I rocked against him.

I whimpered, desperate for my release as Damien pulled his mouth back from me and pushed to his feet. His hands went to his pants, and he tugged them down, freeing his thick cock.

"Damien, we can't."

He pushed the head of himself against my clit. "This," his mouth hovered over mine as his ragged breathing fanned over my face, and I could smell my own excitement on his lips. "is mine." He rocked his hips forward. "Tell me your pussy belongs to me, princess."

I bit down on my lip to suppress a moan. "It's yours."

He spun me around and pushed me forward, so my hands landed on the bed as he grabbed my hips and positioned his cock against my entrance from behind. I groaned as he slid into me, fucking me fast.

"I want you sore. I want you to feel me every time you move." He continued to pump into me, his fingers gripping my hips so tightly they would leave bruises, marking me.

Leaning down over me, his lips went to my ear, and he whispered, "I want your cunt filled with my seed."

Those words sent me over the edge, and I clenched down on his length. One of his hands covered my mouth, muffling my cries as he continued ramming into me. After several more pumps, he filled me, and his juices leaked from my slit, coating my thighs.

"Such a good fucking girl," He praised me, turning me to face him so he could claim my mouth with his. His fingers found my clit, and he rubbed my little nub in circles, drawing out another orgasm. My legs felt week, and my pussy was full of cream that would drip from me with every spasm of my body. "Now hurry up and get dressed. The sooner we get dinner over with, the sooner I can bury my cock in you."

With that, he pressed a small kiss to my forehead and slipped back out into the hallway.

TWENTY-TWO

DAMIEN

Slipping into Valerie's room while her mother and ex were here was dangerous. But I couldn't keep my hands off her, and I needed to know where we stood.

I hurried and got dressed so my little princess wouldn't be forced to spend time alone with Chase. I knew exactly what kind of guy that prick was.

He thought everyone owed him something, and his money bought him respect. But that couldn't be farther from the way I lived my life. Respect was earned, and if I wanted something, I went out and worked hard for it. I didn't let my father hand me anything.

I hurried downstairs and sank down on a stool at the island. Chase was soon leaning against the other side in a polo shirt and khakis. He eyed my jeans and t-shirt with disapproval.

"How long have you been here?" he asked, his eyes studying me.

I shrugged. "Few days." I figured the vaguer I was, the better.

"You're a soldier, right?"

I nodded. "What is it you do?"

He smirked. "A little of this, a little of that." That was code for nothing. He didn't do anything.

"How long are you in town for?" I asked.

"Just long enough for Valerie to pack."

That response made my spine stiffen. "I didn't get the impression she'd forgiven you."

"You know how it is. I'll buy her a bracelet, and she'll be fine."

"No, I don't know how it is. I wouldn't cheat on Valerie."

His eyes narrowed. "Of course you wouldn't because she's your sister."

"*Stepsister*," I corrected just as Pam entered the room wearing a gold sequin top and hot pants with heels.

"You boys ready to go? Where is Valerie?"

"I'll go get her," Chase replied a little too quickly as his gaze landed on me with a smirk.

I forced myself to stay on the stool and not follow after him. But I didn't need to. A few seconds later, a door slammed, and Valerie was making her way down the stairs with Chase close behind her.

I pushed from my seat and turned to look at her, momentarily breathless as I took her in. She wore a hot pink dress that came to the top of her thighs and sandals.

I wondered if she had panties on underneath and if her thighs were sticky from my cum. Her face began to heat when she looked at me, and she quickly averted her gaze.

"I'll drive," Chase blurted out. I didn't know if he thought that would impress Pam, but I wasn't going to argue with him. I didn't need to get into a pissing contest with this idiot. I'd already won. So instead, I made sure Pam sat in the passenger seat of her luxury SUV so I could be in the back with Valerie. She sat behind Chase, and I eyed her thighs, cocking an eyebrow. Her cheeks darkened, and she turned to look out of the window.

"So, Damien," Chase called out, looking at me through the rearview mirror. "How do you like Pam's place here?"

"It's nice," I looked over at Valerie again, who seemed tense every time he spoke.

"We are thinking of having our wedding here, aren't we, baby?"

"We talked about this," she bit out.

"Valerie, you are not going to throw away your future over one little mistake," Pam added.

"What if it's not the future she wants?" I asked.

The car went silent before her mother cleared her throat. "It's the future she deserves," Pam replied.

Valerie snorted. "What did I ever do to you?"

That made me laugh as Chase and Pam exchanged a look. "Damien, when did you say you were heading back to the base?"

"I have a few more days until I need to sign in."

"After all this traveling I've been doing, it will be so nice to have a nice quiet place to relax for a while."

That was stepmother code for *get the fuck out*. I bit back a curse and nodded.

"I can be gone by morning."

I didn't look over at Valerie. I couldn't.

"I'm not trying to rush you –"

"It's no problem. I have a lot to take care of anyway," I lied.

***

Dinner was a complete shitshow. We barely said a word as we pushed pretentious food around our plates. The only person who seemed happy was Chase, who was grinning like the cat who got the cream.

At least Chase was sleeping in a guest room. So I didn't have to worry about him putting his hands on Valerie. I waited as long as I could until about three in the morning before I snuck into her bedroom. She was asleep curled on her side. Her eyes looked puffy, and her face was pink like she'd been crying. I ran the back of my knuckles across her cheek, and her eyes blinked open.

"Hey, princess."

She pushed up, wrapping her arms around my neck and pulling me against her. I let my arms loop around her as well and squeezed her to my chest.

TWENTY-THREE

VALERIE

I knew Damien wouldn't be staying long, but I wasn't prepared for how much I'd care that he was leaving. I hugged him against me, wishing he could take me with him.

"We don't have much time, sweetheart, he whispered into my hair as he pulled back from me, his lips finding mine. "I'm sorry this is how it's ending."

His words caused a fracture in my chest, and all I could do is nod. Then, pushing my hair back from my face, his eyes searched mine. "I can hold you for a while."

"No," I blurted out a little too quickly. "I want to be with you." If this was my last night with him, and possibly the only person I'd be with before I was ultimately forced into a marriage with someone I couldn't love, I wanted to make it count.

I sat up further, pushing his shoulder and swinging a leg over him to straddle him. My mouth found his, and I rocked against him, eliciting a moan from the back of his throat. His cock went hard, and he lifted me from him, sitting me back on my bed before he tugged his shirt off and shoved down his shorts.

I watched as he fisted his cock, slipping out of my own clothes and laying back on the bed with my legs spread for him. He looked down at me like I was the most beautiful thing he'd ever seen before, sliding his hand down my thigh to push me open further. He pressed his lips against my skin, slowly working his way down toward my center.

I raised my hips, but he put his palm on my lower stomach and pushed me back down. His lips went to my other leg, and he peppered kissed against my flesh until I was dripping wet and desperate for him to touch me.

"I love how your body responds to me," he whispered before placing a soft kiss on my clit. His tongue ran out over my slit and he spread me open and pushed his tongue into my entrance.

"I love what you do to my body," I replied as I rocked against his face. Then, pressing a finger inside of me, he began to slowly pump it in and out of me as he latched on to my clit. "Oh God," I cried out as my orgasm hit me fast.

He licked me clean until every last quiver of pleasure rolled through me.

"I want you to ride my cock, princess." He laid on his back, gripping his base. I crawled over him, running my tongue along the head of his cock before positioning him beneath my entrance. Slowly, I sank down, taking his tip inside of me. He hissed at the contact, and it emboldened me to sink lower. His hands went to my hips, grabbing hold of me as he lifted himself to put his dick all the way inside of me. "I need to feel you," he groaned, pulling me down, so my chest was against his.

I began to ride him, clinging to his body like he was going to disappear. I pushed the thought from my mind, letting myself get lost in the pleasure. He placed a palm on either side of my face and guided my lips to his, fucking my mouth with his tongue as I rode him.

"I can't get enough of you," he whispered against my mouth. My body clenched down on him, and his cock swelled as he pumped into me from below.

His lips were on mine again, swallowing my cries of pleasure as we both came undone.

Damien pressed a kiss to my lips, then another before holding me tightly against him.

***

I awoke alone, my heart racing as my hand slid over my bed. I threw on my clothing and rushed from my room and down the hallway, yanking open Damien's door. He was gone. His room was empty. My heart sank.

TWENTY-FOUR

DAMIEN

I couldn't say goodbye to her. It was bad enough I was being forced to leave, and Chase would be there with her.

I couldn't understand the ache in my chest as I drove across the state line. I knew it was going to end this way. I just thought I had a few more days.

I reached the base just as night started to fall. At least all of the work I had to do around here would keep me busy, and I hoped it was enough to forget her.

The plan had always been to get out and start my own business. I loved cars. Fixing them up and making them faster was what I'd wanted to do since I was little. My father had other plans for me, so I took my future into my own hands and joined the military. But now, it was time to move on.

***

There wasn't a day I didn't think of her. When my father called and told me that his marriage to Pam had fallen apart after three weeks gone, it gave me hope that maybe one day I would see her again. But two weeks later, when I got an invitation to Chase and Valerie's wedding, I knew I could never go back.

I walked away from the Army and used the money I had saved, along with a loan, to open my own car shop in a small town in Pennsylvania.

It took me a few months to get on my feet, but soon, I was booked up for months. My income was steady, and I was living out my dream. Well, what had once been my dream, but when I laid my head down at night, the only thing I saw was Valerie.

A horn honked in the parking lot, and I shoved my shop rag into my back pocket and trudged out toward the Chevelle that seemed to be eager to get my attention. The man inside rolled down his window and began asking me about some custom alterations for his interior with a thick Boston accent.

"Best I can do is four months."

"I need this done in a couple of weeks. We're going to a car show in Richmond."

"Sorry, I can't help you out. Maybe Fuller's down in Shrewsberry can help you out."

"But you do the best work in the state."

I grinned. I couldn't help it. "That's why I'm booked up. You want it done fast, or do you want it done right?"

"Good things come to those who wait. Isn't that the saying?" A woman called out from behind me.

I spun around, my eyes landing on Valerie before lowering to her large belly.

"Yeah, alright. I'll bring it back in a couple months," the man grumbled, but I was already walking away from him.

"What are you doing here?" I asked, desperate to touch her but forcing myself to keep my distance.

"I needed to see you."

My eyes went to her stomach. "Where's your husband?"

"I'm not married."

"I got the invitation –"

"My mom sent those out. I left the day after you did, alone."

"Then," my eyes fell again, and I took a tentative step closer to her. "Is it —" I couldn't even finish my sentence.

Grabbing my hand and pressing it against her belly, she nodded, tears springing to her eyes. "It's ours."

I wrapped my arms around her, lifting her from the ground as I buried my head against her neck. I'd missed her smell, the feel of her soft skin against mine.

I lowered her back to the ground, reluctantly loosening my grip on her so I could look at her face.

"You're a hard man to track down."

"I didn't want to be found," I confessed.

She winced. "You mean you didn't want *me* to find you."

"It was easier not to see your face, except for when I went to sleep at night, princess." I pushed her hair back from her face, rubbing my thumb along her cheek. She leaned into my touch like she had been just as desperate to be close to me as I had been.

"Have you –" she swallowed, shaking her head. "Did you find someone else?"

"Since the moment I saw you in that tub, there never could have been anyone else for me, princess." Her mouth pressed against mine, and I slid my fingers into her hair as I deepened our kiss, my other hand on her belly.

EPILOGUE

VALERIE

I relaxed back in the tub, rubbing my hand over my swollen belly before putting some peach body wash on a bath scrunchie and rubbing it over my skin.

"I could help you with that," my husband called from the doorway before sauntering closer. I handed the sponge to him as his mouth met mine, kissing me deeply as he rubbed the scratchy material over my breast, causing my nipple to harden.

"Isn't this how we got into this mess in the first place?" I asked as he rubbed down over my stomach and dipped his fingers between my legs.

"DJ is finally down for a nap, and if we don't get some alone time now, I won't be able to have you until bedtime."

"You're dirty talk sure has gotten lame over the years," I teased, thankful Damien Junior was finally out for a while so I could relax.

"You're still such a little brat," he groaned as he rubbed over my clit. I whimpered, but his hand left me, and he continued to wash me, taking his time to make sure every inch of me was clean. "This scent is making me hungry."

"Why do you think I got this soap?" I asked, raising an eyebrow at him.

"Such a tease," he shot back as he held out his hand for me. I took it, allowing him to pull me from the tub.

"I want you on the bed on your knees," he ordered as he shoved down his pants and kicked them off before gripping his cock in his hand.

I climbed up onto the mattress on all fours, and Damien came up behind me, rubbing his tongue against my slit before pumping two fingers inside me. "You're always so wet for me," he growled. "I love how fucking sexy you look on your knees, swollen with my baby."

He walked around the bed, reaching over and palming a tit, giving it a little squeeze before he walked around to face me, stroking his length.

In his other hand, he held out a peach, and I couldn't help the wicked smile that spread across my face.

"Take a bite, princess."

I bit down into the fruit, juice dripping from my lips. "Now get on your back and spread your legs so I can have a taste too."

I didn't hesitate, laying down in the center of the bed with my legs spread wide. Damien climbed up between them, taking the half-eaten fruit and rubbing it over my clit as he licked every drop of juice from me. And then, he ate the peach while I rode his cock, like the good girl he taught me to be.

THE END

ABOUT THE AUTHOR

Nova Monroe is a saucy little minx who loves to write about dirty and forbidden things.

Email: AuthorNovaMonroe@yahoo.com

Twitter: @MsNovaMonroe

Instagram: AuthorNovaMonroe

Website: AuthorNovaMonroe.com

Facebook: Nova Monroe

WHAT TO READ NEXT

Hard Knox – I knew today would be no different from any other. Not a single person remembered that it was my birthday. I thought about skipping school altogether, but I was already falling behind in Algebra and was dangerously close to failing for the year. The last thing I wanted was to be a senior again. I needed to graduate so I could move as far away from this place as possible and start a new life. There was only one thing standing in the way of my goal, and that was Mr. Knox.

CONTAINS: STUDENT/TEACHER & M/F/M

Tainted - I met Jonas at the gym. We both loved to work out and eat right, causing us to become fast friends. That's the lie we tell everyone anyway. How we really met would raise a few eyebrows, and it wasn't the kind of thing you bring up in casual conversations on the golf course. We were the type of friends who barbequed at each other's homes on the weekends, and I was going to be the best man at his wedding. What we did on Wednesdays is what may make people cringe when they look at us and would definitely cause Jonas to have to see a divorce lawyer. It all started out with a bet, a drunken dare that I couldn't back down from.

THIS BOOK CONTAINS: M/M & M/F/M

www.ingramcontent.com/pod-product-compliance
Lightning Source LLC
Chambersburg PA
CBHW071626150726
48000CB00004B/1901

9798536340042